# DRAGONBREATH

## LAIR OF THE BAT MONSTER

# DRAGONBREATH
## LAIR OF THE BAT MONSTER

### BY
## URSULA VERNON

DIAL  BOOKS

an imprint of Penguin Group (USA) Inc.

*This one's for all the friends and readers working in animal rescue whose stories have kept me entertained and given me hope over the years. From homicidal eagles to surly wombats and spiky puggles— I'm so glad you're out there.*

DIAL BOOKS
An imprint of Penguin Group (USA) Inc.
Published by The Penguin Group • Penguin Group (USA) Inc., 375 Hudson Street, New York, NY 10014, U.S.A. • Penguin Group (Canada), 90 Eglinton Avenue East, Suite 700, Toronto, Ontario, Canada M4P 2Y3 (a division of Pearson Penguin Canada Inc.) • Penguin Books Ltd, 80 Strand, London WC2R 0RL, England • Penguin Ireland, 25 St. Stephen's Green, Dublin 2, Ireland (a division of Penguin Books Ltd) • Penguin Group (Australia), 250 Camberwell Road, Camberwell, Victoria 3124, Australia (a division of Pearson Australia Group Pty Ltd) Penguin Books India Pvt Ltd, 11 Community Centre, Panchsheel Park, New Delhi - 110 017, India • Penguin Group (NZ), 67 Apollo Drive, Rosedale, North Shore 0632, New Zealand (a division of Pearson New Zealand Ltd) • Penguin Books (South Africa) (Pty) Ltd, 24 Sturdee Avenue, Rosebank, Johannesburg 2196, South Africa • Penguin Books Ltd, Registered Offices: 80 Strand, London WC2R 0RL, England

Designed by Jennifer Kelly
Text set in Stempel Schneidler
Printed in the U.S.A.

10 9 8 7 6 5 4 3 2 1

Library of Congress Cataloging-in-Publication Data
Vernon, Ursula.
Dragonbreath: lair of the bat monster / by Ursula Vernon    p. cm.
Summary: When Danny and Wendell find an injured bat at the neighborhood pool, they take it to Mexico, where Danny's cousin, a bat specialist, lives, but once there Danny is snatched up by a giant bat monster, and it is up to Wendell to save him.
  ISBN 978-0-8037-3525-5
[1. Adventure and adventurers—Fiction. 2. Dragons—Fiction. 3. Iguanas—Fiction.
4. Bats—Fiction. 5. Mexico—Fiction.]
  PZ7.V5985 Lai 2011
  [Fic]—dc22        2010012143

THE DEEPEST JUNGLE. THE DARK HEART OF
THE RAIN FOREST. THE BRAVE EXPLORER FIGHTS
HIS WAY THROUGH THE UNDERGROWTH.

HE HAS LOST MOST OF HIS TEAM TO MALARIA, HOSTILE NATIVES, AND WILD BEASTS. ONLY HIS FAITHFUL PORTER, BWANA WENDELL, REMAINS.

BUT AT LAST, HIS GOAL IS IN SIGHT!

# STRANGE DISCOVERY

"It's really hot," said Wendell. "I want to get in the pool. Is there some reason you're standing there mumbling?"

Danny Dragonbreath started. "Oh! Uh. No, I was just . . ." He waved a hand vaguely. "You know. Uh."

Wendell sighed. He did indeed know. The iguana had been Danny's best friend through several grades, multiple emergency room visits, and countless daydreams.

"The jungle is really cool," Danny announced.

Wendell looked around. They were standing on the edge of the neighborhood pool. There were a few potted plants around the pool, and a hedge on the other side of the chain-link fence, but nothing that could really be called a jungle.

"I think the heat has addled your brain."

Danny scoffed. "Heat doesn't bother me. I'm a dragon."

"I have this vague memory of going to the beach with you last summer . . ."

"Um."

"You sunburned so badly you couldn't sleep on your back for a week."

OH, *ONE TIME!*

Danny sighed with relief. He'd promised his mom he'd wear sunscreen—she hadn't forgotten the Beach Incident either—but he never remembered to bring it. There were so many things to think about, and so many things to remember. He was usually lucky if he remembered a towel.

"Say, Wendell . . ."

"I brought a towel for you too."

It was a warm day. Several families were out swimming. Big Eddy the Komodo dragon, the neighborhood bully, was lurking in the deep end of the pool.

Wendell sat down on the edge and put a toe gingerly into the water. "Brrrrr . . ." He began inching down the steps.

Danny, being Danny, got a running start and cannonballed into the pool.

"GERONIMO!"

"NOOOOO!"

"It's faster this way," said Danny, treading water with his tail. "Besides, it's like a hundred degrees out. Doesn't that feel *great*?"

Wendell muttered something unkind. An older gecko who had been sunbathing sat up and glared at Danny.

"Um. Sorry," said Danny. "Didn't see you there."

She grumbled, and lay back down.

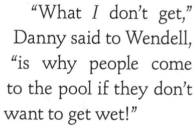

"What *I* don't get," Danny said to Wendell, "is why people come to the pool if they don't want to get wet!"

Wendell might have had an excellent explanation, but he was too busy staring at something rising out of the water behind Danny.

"Oh, well, if you're getting out, don't let us stop you," said Danny, stepping aside.

Big Eddy looked baffled, then enraged. He loomed over the much smaller dragon.

Danny glanced around the pool. There were three adults, not including the sunbathing gecko. Big Eddy wasn't going to pound him flat in front of grown-ups, no matter how much he might want to. At the moment, Danny was safe, and he knew it.

Big Eddy knew it too. The Komodo dragon shoved by him, "accidentally" pushing his elbow into Danny's side, and stomped away.

An hour or two later, exhausted from swimming and splashing and playing Marco Polo, Wendell and Danny floated lazily in the pool. The families had left, the sunbathing gecko had rolled up her towel, and it was just the two boys and the sparkling blue water.

Danny rolled over to float on his back. It would be months until school started again. The pool was open every day. Could life get any better?

The clouds were all kinds of interesting shapes. Danny could see a rocket and a gun and something that might be a giant squid. He squinted. Definitely a giant squid. And the wind was moving, so the giant squid was reaching for the gun and that cloud over there could be a cowboy, and they could have an epic shootout—

"What's that?" asked Wendell.

"It's a giant squid with a—"

"Don't mention giant squid," said Wendell, and shuddered. He'd come entirely too close to one last year, courtesy of one of Danny's crazy schemes. "And I don't know what you're talking about, but I'm talking about *that.*"

The iguana pointed. Danny paddled over to see what he was looking at.

There was something in the pool filter, in the little alcove where water flowed in and out. It looked like a black clump of leaves.

"Is it leaves?" Danny peered closer.

"I don't think leaves try to climb things."

As they watched, the black lump hitched itself against the wall and scrabbled faintly, then dropped back into the water.

"I think it's a bat!" said Danny, astonished.

Wendell fumbled for one of the towels by the edge of the pool and wiped the water off his glasses. "Huh. I think you're right."

Wendell screwed his face up in thought. Danny waited. Wendell was a nerd down to his toenails, and every bit of information he learned stayed stuck in his brain, like lint stuck to a lump of clay after you rolled it across the carpet.*

"We're not supposed to touch it," said Wendell finally. "We need gloves or something."

"But it's *tiny*," said Danny. "What's it going to do to us?"

IT MIGHT HAVE RABIES!

OOH, LIKE THE FOAMING AT THE MOUTH KIND?

*Danny's mother had been very annoyed by this experiment, and Danny's explanation that he was trying to invent a new way of sweeping did not help matters.

"I don't think there's another kind of rabies," said Wendell. "If you get one of the towels, we can catch it in that."

Danny grabbed a towel and wrapped it around his hand. He reached into the alcove.

"Be careful," said Wendell, hovering nervously behind him. "I think they're really fragile. But don't let it bite you. Remember the were-wieners . . ."

"Aw, c'mon. That was *cool*." Danny couldn't fit his whole body into the alcove, so he put his cheek against the pool's edge and groped around blind.

"You're nearly there," said Wendell, looking over his shoulder.

Danny's towel-covered fingers closed over something that was only a little more solid than air. "Got it!"

He pulled out the black lump.

"It's so light!" said Danny.

"They have to be, to fly," said Wendell, shoving his glasses up on his nose.

They looked at the bat. It had a short, dog-like muzzle and gigantic ears with big flaps of skin in

them. Its mouth was slightly open, revealing a fine fringe of teeth.

"It's . . . kinda . . . cute. In a hideous sort of way."

"Yeah," said Wendell. "Kinda . . . ugly cute . . . ish . . ."

"So what kind of bat is it?"

"It was a two-page report," said Wendell. "I didn't get into advanced bat taxonomy."

"Well, why doesn't it fly away, then?" asked Danny. "You! Bat! Go on!"

The bat sat there.

"I don't think it can," said Wendell. "It looks pretty waterlogged. And is that a hole in its wing?"

The iguana poked gingerly at the bat's wing. It pulled the wing back and made a noise.

"Yeeeek!" Wendell fell over backward, and even Danny jumped.

It wasn't a noise that an animal would make. It was an angry staticky chatter, like a furious radio. Danny had never heard anything like it.

"What's it saying?"

"I don't know! I don't speak bat!" Wendell picked himself up. "Maybe we should leave it somewhere, let it dry out . . ."

"Well, what are we going to do?"

Danny, moving very slowly, flipped the towel over the top of the bat. It didn't react. "I don't know . . . but I know who will."

He made a small, awkward bundle of bat and towel. The bat wasn't moving around. He hoped it could breathe.

"Let's take it to Mom."

# A BATTY COUSIN

There is a particular tone of voice that strikes fear and terror into the hearts of parents everywhere, a kind of studied nonchalance that means something has gone horribly, horribly wrong, and Danny was using it.

"Saaaaaaaaay, Mom?"

Mrs. Dragonbreath froze. She turned slowly in her office chair, sniffing the air. She couldn't smell smoke. At least, not a lot of smoke. The house usually smelled faintly smoky—dragons lived there, after all—but there wasn't the smell she'd expect if, say, the house was on fire. That was something, at least.

"Yeeeeeeessssssss?" she said.

Danny stood in the doorway. Wendell was behind him, apparently walking under his own power, so that ruled out "severely injured Wendell," which had been the source of that tone several times in the past. ("Saaaaaaay, Mom...if...y'know,

just hypothetically . . . somebody had dislocated their arm, what exactly would it look like?")

"You remember that bird we found last spring?" asked Danny.

"The robin? Yes . . ."

Danny held out a towel-wrapped bundle. "We found a bat in the swimming pool. We think it's hurt. Can you help it?"

"Um," said Danny's mother. She took the towel gingerly. "A bat? Don't they carry rabies?"

"We were very careful," said Wendell. "We only handled it through the towel."

"Um."

"You were really good with the bird!" said Danny eagerly. "I'm sure you can help this bat!"

"Your confidence is touching," said his mother dryly. She picked the knotted towel apart with her claws and folded it back. The bat looked up at her with small, bright eyes.

"You can do something, right?" said Danny, leaning forward.

"I don't know . . . All I did was put the bird in a dark box and take it to the wildlife rescue people. And birds don't get rabies."

"But *Mom* . . ."

She looked at him. Danny tried to look sad and earnest and hopeful, an expression that occasionally worked on his mother.

She snorted once, loudly, steam rising from her nostrils. "Don't give me that look."

His mother gazed into the small, scrunched-up face of the bat, like a mouse-sized gargoyle—a face that only a mother could love.

She sighed. Danny knew from long experience that

that particular sigh indicated surrender. "Fine. I don't know much about bats myself, but I know who does."

"Who?" asked Danny.

"Your cousin Steve. He's some kind of bat researcher down in Mexico. If you can find a cardboard box to keep your little friend in, I'll give your cousin a call."

"Thanks, Mom!" Danny turned to bolt out of the room, paused, made sure Wendell wasn't looking, and gave his mom a quick hug. "You're the best!"

"I'm a sucker is what I am," muttered his mother, but she smiled anyway.

By the time Danny and Wendell had located a cardboard box, Danny's mother was on the phone, and the conversation was one of those one-sided grown-up ones that are frustrating to try to listen to.

"Uh-huh. . . . Uh-huh. . . . Got it. . . . You're sure it's no trouble? . . . Uh-huh. . . ."

Danny and Wendell waited impatiently while Mrs. Dragonbreath wrote on a notepad. Danny poked his head over the counter to see what she was writing. It said "Pillowcase" and "East Whitton Station, Mexico," and then she'd apparently run out of things to write and was doodling flowers and cartoon chickens all over the pad.

"Thanks, Steve," said Mrs. Dragonbreath finally. "I know it'll mean a lot to them. Talk to you later."

She hung up the phone. "Okay. Steve says to bring your bat down to him and he'll see what he can do." She frowned at the towel-wrapped bat. "And we're supposed to put him in a pillowcase, not a box, so he has something to cling to."

Danny ran for a pillowcase. By the time he came back, his mother was counting out change on the counter.

"It's a long bus ride. Nearly two hours. Steve says it's okay if you stay overnight, so make sure you pack a toothbrush."

MRS. DRAGONBREATH, DOES THE FACT THAT WE'RE TAKING A BUS TO MEXICO SEEM A LITTLE *ODD* TO YOU?

IT'S A GOOD BUS SYSTEM. WHY?

Danny's mom waved. "Now, don't make any trouble for your cousin Steve. He's very busy with his research."

"Yes, Mom . . ."

"And don't get bitten by any bats!"

# INTO THE JUNGLE

It was a long bus ride. Wendell knew that Mexico was a long ways off, and even Danny's bizarre bus-ride-bending field—or whatever it was that allowed him to take buses to places like mythical Japan and the Sargasso Sea—seemed to have trouble with it.

They changed buses twice, once at the mall terminal, and once in a place Wendell had never seen, which was very dusty and full of chickens. Somebody came out and played mariachi music at them, but went away after Danny started to sing along.

TIJUANA – 47 MILES

They passed the time reading comic books. Wendell had brought the latest issue of *Empire of Feathers,* and Danny was reading *Single-Cell Samurai,* about a heroic blood cell bitten by radioactive bacteria, which traveled the land fighting monsters and Righting Wrongs.

At last the bus pulled off the dusty highway onto a very dusty gravel road, and then onto a road that was nothing *but* dust, surrounded on all sides by dense vegetation. It looked like a jungle, and it was a much greener green than the parks near Wendell's house.

The bus stopped. "East Whitton Station," said the bus driver.

Danny stuffed his comic back in his backpack, picked up the pillowcase with the bat in it, and hopped off the bus. Wendell followed.

The humidity hit them like a wall. It was hot and wet, in ways that redefined "hot" and "wet." Wendell felt like he was standing in a shower with his clothes on.

NO...
IT'S LIKE
WALKING INTO
SOMEBODY'S
ARMPIT.

EWWW.

Once the bus had rumbled away, the buzz of insects grew louder and louder. A cicada the size of Wendell's arm peered down at them from a high twig and clattered its wings.

"Cousin Steve's supposed to meet us here . . ." said Danny, turning in a circle. "Wow, can you imagine working out here? It's so cool!"

"It's awfully . . . buggy . . ." said Wendell. He swatted at a bug on his arm. "Oh god! It bit me!"

IT'S JUST A MOSQUITO...

WHAT IF IT HAD MALARIA? OR SLEEPING SICKNESS! OR BURULI ULCER! I HAVEN'T HAD SHOTS!

MAN, TOO BAD IT'S SUMMER. YOU COULD GET OUT OF SCHOOL FOR A MONTH!

"It might have malaria," said a voice behind them, "but sleeping sickness is African. And how did you even *hear* about Buruli ulcer?"

"I read a lot," said Wendell defensively. "And it's a horrible disease! You get a sore on your shoulder and then your arm falls off!"

Danny had to admit that this was pretty neat. Well, probably not the bit where your arm actually fell off, but still . . .

"And if you get the sore on your neck, your head falls off!"

"Cool!" said Danny.

"It's really not likely . . ." said the newcomer.

Another mosquito buzzed by Wendell. The iguana yelped and flung his arms over his head.

"Ignore him," said Danny. "Wendell's just paranoid ever since he got ly—lycan—werewolfiness a while ago. You must be my cousin Steve!"

Danny's cousin wasn't like any dragon Wendell had ever seen, and after several years as Danny's best friend, he'd seen quite a few. For one thing,

Steve wasn't much taller than the iguana himself. Instead of spikes, he had a mane of colorful feathers around his head, and in a poof at the tip of his tail.

"And you must be Danny." Steve grinned. "Is that the patient in the pillowcase?"

"Oh! Yes!" Danny held out the pillowcase. Steve held up his hands.

"No, no. You hold on to him, at least until we're on the boat."

"We're going on a boat?" asked Wendell.

"Of course," said Steve. "My research station's upriver."

They set off into the brush, following Steve. Wendell might have argued, but the mosquitoes were attacking in force now, like a flying squadron of hypodermic needles. He was going to get a horrible disease. Possibly more than one. His limbs were going to fall off. They might be falling off *right now!*

Wendell wondered briefly which was worse—the notion of his arms falling off or the fact that Steve and Danny apparently had a similar sense of humor.

"I've got bug spray at my station," said Steve, taking pity on him. "If you can keep everything attached until we get there, we should be able to keep the mosquitoes off you."

"C'mon!" said Danny. Wendell sighed, hugging himself tightly to present the smallest target possible to insects.

They trudged after Steve. The green wall of the jungle closed behind them.

The trip up the river to Steve's research station was hot, wet, and terrifying.

The boat was low in the water, and occasionally water slopped in over the sides. And it was made of rubber, which seemed horrifyingly flimsy to Wendell—wasn't the river full of sharp rocks? Couldn't piranhas bite through it? Why were the nature shows always concerned about how fast a school of piranhas could skeletonize a cow, when obviously it was how fast they could skeletonize a *boat* that was really important?

And there were creeper vines hanging low over the river that dragged across the back of your neck, and might have any sort of biting bug on them, or which might actually be snakes. And not *people*-snakes, like the Gorskys down the road or Ms. Brown the English teacher—but real wild primitive snakes that couldn't talk or think or wear clothes, and ate their food in one gulp. *Animals.*

Those were the terrifying bits.

But even Wendell had to admit that the awesome bits were pretty awesome. The jungle pressed in over the river, and there were wonderfully vivid birds leaping across the tree branches, in colors that Wendell had never seen outside a crayon box. Steve knew most of their names, too. A head as big as Danny's fists broke out of the water, trailing a V-shaped wake, and turned out to be a giant otter, which looked at them with soulful black eyes before diving again.

And best of all was when they came around a bend and Steve cut the engine, said "Look!" and pointed out a family of snouty, grunting animals that had come down to the water to drink.

"What are they?" breathed Danny.

"Tapirs!" said Wendell.

Steve nodded. "Baird's tapirs. They're endangered, although there are still a lot of them around here." He waited until the tapirs had finished drinking and vanished into the forest before firing up the outboard motor again. "Natives call them *cash-i-tzimin*, the jungle horse. I'm so glad we saw them!"

That was the thing about Steve. Wendell had to admit that Danny's cousin was . . . well . . . *cool.* He got excited about things, not like most adults. He was pointing out birds like a little kid with trading cards, and he was just as thrilled by the otter and the tapirs as Danny and Wendell were.

Plus, he'd cut through the undergrowth back to the boat with a machete. *And* he'd let Danny try it. Wendell wasn't entirely comfortable with Danny having large sharp objects, but it was still *cool.*

Danny's parents were pretty laid-back as parents go, but even they drew the line at sharp objects, particularly after the incident with the homemade guillotine and the trail of headless action figures.*

"Are there lots of endangered animals around here?" asked Danny.

Steve frowned, and looked like a grown-up for the first time since meeting them. "Some days it seems like they're *all* endangered. And I'm trying to get more added to the endangered list, but it's slow going."

"More added?"

"My bats," Steve explained. "There's a big cave full of them that I'm trying to protect. I'm afraid someone will go in, maybe with dynamite, and start blasting, looking for gold or something. There's lots of mining around here."

---

*Wendell's SuperSkink (Now with death lasso and authentic kung-fu grip!) had never been the same after his beheading, but Wendell had never liked SuperSkink's expression anyway. **45**

I CAN'T IMAGINE DYNAMITE IS GOOD FOR THE BATS.

GENERALLY NOT, NO.

CAN'T THEY JUST FLY AWAY?

"Well, some of them would, if the blast didn't get them outright. But this is a great cave! Bats have been roosting there and raising babies for thousands of years! And it doesn't seem right to blow up their home just to find a little bit of gold or bauxite or whatever the miners are looking for."

Danny considered this. He wouldn't want anybody blowing up his bedroom looking for gold. Admittedly, he'd once dug up part of the backyard looking for pirate treasure, but all he'd located was something called a septic tank, and that had ended badly.*

"The poor bats!" he said. "How do we help them?"

Steve stared up at a patch of sky between the trees. "Well, that's the problem. They're all common species, so I can't prove that there's any reason to save the cave."

*He'd been grounded for a month, and they'd had to spend three days at a hotel until the stink died down. Danny had definitely learned his lesson on that one, which was that digging for gold was a bad idea.

"The jungle's huge!" Steve waved his arms in the air. "And it's full of things nobody's ever seen! There are bugs and birds that science has never even heard of, because nobody's ever brought one back and described it!"

"That is so cool!" Danny wondered what it would be like to discover a new bug. He could name it after himself. Or Wendell. Or maybe his mother . . . yeah, that was probably a good idea, particularly if it was something like a butterfly. It never hurt to get some credit built up, so the next time he got in a scrape, Mom would think of her very own butterfly, and she'd let him off with a warning instead of grounding him.

It would have to be pretty, though. A hideous chewing parasite, however interesting, probably wouldn't work. Mom was pretty cool for a mom, but in Danny's experience, few girls appreciated being given the gift of lice.

"Anyway," said Steve, "if I can find a new species, the government will have to protect the cave so people can study it. So that's what I'm looking for out here."

A bug the size of Wendell's hand landed on the prow of the boat and looked at Wendell. Wendell looked back.

It didn't look like it could bite, but Wendell wasn't taking any chances. Possibly it could sting, or spit, or make unkind personal remarks. "Go away," he told the bug.

The bug ignored him. Wendell huddled in the bottom of the boat and held his tail firmly to make sure it didn't fall off.

Fortunately Steve's research station came into view before the giant bug attacked. Steve pulled the boat up to the dock and cut the motor. "Well, here we are: Whitton Station! Come on in!"

"Are there bats inside?" asked Danny, holding tight to the pillowcase with its single passenger.

"Lots," said Steve. "All kinds. Come on in, I'll introduce you to some of my favorites!"

Wendell inched past the menacing bug on the prow and onto the pier. He weighed the possibility of rabies vs. whatever tropical diseases the bugs might carry, gulped, and followed Danny and Steve up the walkway to the house.

# MEET THE BATS!

The inside of Steve's research station was dimly lit and dreadfully cluttered. Paper was stacked up on every available surface, forming columns that fell over and became sliding piles. On top of those piles were Steve's plastic tubs and trays. (Some of the tubs were labeled MEALWORMS. Wendell gave them a wide berth.)

Big cages of chicken wire crossed the walls, with dark

shapes hanging from the tops, and there was a pegboard with several pillowcases hung from it. A couple of the pillowcases were moving.

"Now!" said Steve, clearing a spot on a large plywood table. "Let's see the patient."

Danny carefully laid the pillowcase down on the table. Steve pulled on a pair of gloves and folded back the cloth, revealing the bedraggled black bat.

"Well?" asked Danny, peering curiously over his cousin's shoulder.

"He's a big brown bat," Steve said, carefully stretching out one of the bat's wings. The bat didn't resist. Inasmuch as its little scrunched face had any expression, Wendell would have said that the bat was sulking.

"He doesn't *look* very big . . ."

"No, no, that's the name of the species. There

are . . . oh . . . evening bats and false vampire bats and Mexican free-tailed bats. This one's a big brown bat. There are little brown bats that are even smaller."

"Are his wings okay?" Danny wanted to know. "There's that hole in them . . ."

Steve nodded. "They look okay. Nothing seems broken. He might have had that hole for a while too—it'll close up on its own, given time." He carefully picked the bat up between gloved fingers and turned it over.

The bat, pushed too far, sank tiny fangs into Steve's glove.

Wendell jumped back. Danny said, "Cool!"

"And this is why I wear gloves . . ." muttered Steve. He carefully checked the bat over, then returned it to the pillowcase. It took a minute to coax the little teeth out of his gloves. "C'mon, little fella, you don't want to hurt your teeth on me . . ."

The bat let out a furious staticky sound. Steve grinned.

"What's that mean?" asked Danny.

"He's very angry," said Steve. He closed the pillowcase and took it over to the pegboard. "You would be too, if you nearly drowned and then got shoved in a sack for hours, and then had a giant monster poking your wings. All that's wrong with him is that he's wet and tired and had a bad day. I'll give him a good meal tonight, and you can take him home tomorrow and let him go."

SO HE'LL BE OKAY?

YEP! AND VERY LUCKY THAT YOU TWO SAVED HIM FROM DROWNING.

LOTS OF BATS GET STUCK IN SWIMMING POOLS AND CAN'T GET OUT AGAIN.

"Hey, what's this?" Wendell wanted to know.

Steve and Danny turned. The iguana was facing an object that looked like a cross between a musical instrument and something you'd slice cheese with.

"Oh, that!" Steve leaned over and plucked one of the tiny strands. "That's a harp trap. Bats fly into it and go sideways to try to avoid the first row of strings, and then they run into the second row. They fall into the little catch down here."

"Does it hurt them?" Wendell wanted to know. The bats might bite, but they were so tiny, it seemed mean to knock them out of the air like that.

"Not at all," Steve assured him. "I mean, they probably don't *enjoy* it, but they don't get hurt. Then I can count how many and what species they are, and tag them and let them go. I promise, I'm trying to save bats, not scar them for life." He took down one of the other pillowcases. "Would you like to see some of them?"

"Sure!"

Steve set the pillowcase down and folded it back, revealing a row of tiny white puffballs. "These are Honduran white bats. They actually make little tents out of big leaves, and hang inside them."

The white bats were absurdly cute. Given how ugly *their* bat was, Danny had pictured most bats as hideous little gargoyles, but the white bats looked like a cross between a piglet and a powder puff.

"They're adorable!" said Danny.

"Yeah." Steve grinned. "This one's not, though . . ." He opened one of the cages and reached in a gloved hand.

"Does it drink blood?" quavered Wendell from behind Danny.

"Nah," said Steve, stroking the ugly creature's head. "Just fruit. They're actually very nice little bats. And the poor things are endangered, too."

Wendell normally would have had a hard time feeling sorry for something with a face like the back end of a crab, but Steve seemed to like it.

Actually, Steve was chucking it under the chin and saying, "Who's a good widdle bat, den? You! Yes, you is!" like Wendell's elderly aunt with her poodle.

It occurred to Wendell that possibly Steve had been living out in the jungle too long.

"Do you have any vampires?" Danny wanted to know. "Do you feed them blood?"

"No, no vampires." Steve put the wrinkled bat away, with a last cuddle. "It's hard to keep blood laying around—you have to mix it with this goop so it doesn't dry out and turn the inside of the feeder into a giant scab—"

Danny rolled his eyes at this blatant show of vocabulary.

"Anyway, vampires are actually pretty harmless. They mostly feed on cows, and the cows don't even notice. They're just like big mosquitoes. Although—this is kinda disgusting and neat—bats have to be really light in order to fly, right?"

"Right," said Danny, who had noticed that their bat hardly weighed anything. Wendell nodded.

"Well, the vampires are so tiny, and blood is mostly liquid, so the bats have to start peeing within two minutes of feeding, just to get rid of all that excess fluid. In one end, and right out the other. It's incredibly efficient. Otherwise they'd be too heavy to fly!"

"Gross!" said Danny, delighted.

"I wish I'd known that for my report," muttered Wendell.

"So I don't keep any vampires. Cleaning up after them is a pain." Steve reached into the last cage. "And anyway, *these* guys are much scarier."

The bat he brought out was enormous. Its wings were almost as long as Wendell's arms, and it had a long, slender muzzle with a little plug of flesh on the end.

"What does he eat?" asked Danny, much impressed.

"Other bats," said Steve with relish.

*"He's a cannibal?"* Wendell asked.

Danny knew immediately what he wanted for Christmas.

"Birds too. He'll drop on them out of the trees and chomp down on their heads. The Zapotec Indians—they used to live around here—worshipped a giant false vampire bat as a god," said Steve. "They called him Camazotz, the lord of bats."

The bat contrived to look smug and somewhat evil.

"I can see why," said Wendell.

"He was the god of night and death and fire," Steve said. "The Zapotec sacrificed prisoners to him."

"You mean *people*?" asked Danny.

"Yup," said Steve. "Sometimes they staged mock wars just to get prisoners to feed to Camazotz."

Steve reluctantly put the false vampire bat away. "Some people think there was an actual giant bat that they worshipped. It's probably extinct, if it ever existed."

Wendell considered the possibility of giant bats flying around eating other bats—and possibly small iguanas—and thought that extinction might be a positive thing in this case.

"I'd love to find one," said Steve wistfully. "Then they'd have to protect my cave."

"Where *is* your cave?" asked Danny.

"Oh!" Steve glanced at the clock. "It's getting late—the bats will be waking up soon. You want to see it?"

"Yes!" said Danny.

"Um," said Wendell.

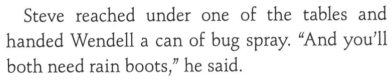

OH COME ON, WENDELL! WHEN ARE WE EVER GONNA SEE A REAL BAT CAVE BACK HOME?

Steve reached under one of the tables and handed Wendell a can of bug spray. "And you'll both need rain boots," he said.

"Rain boots?" asked Wendell faintly.

"The floor of a bat cave is . . . is . . ." Steve waved his hands aimlessly. "Well, you'll see. Look, I think I've got some extras from my last set of interns."

And so, appropriately shod, and reeking of bug spray, the trio tromped out into the darkening jungle.

# CREEPY AND CRAWLY

The jungle was even denser out here, away from the roads, and it was like nothing Danny and Wendell had ever seen.

Danny was used to regular forests, where the trees went up and down, and there were some little low plants and bushes. You had to detour around the bushes, but generally it was like walking in a hall full of pillars, with a distant green ceiling.

The jungle was like a green wall. Every square inch was stuffed with leaf and vine and bark and creeper. There were no trails, no gaps, no breaks. It was just solid, endless green.

FEWER PARROTS IN MY CLOSET, THOUGH.

I THINK.

Steve hacked out a path for them with his machete, slicing back branches and leaves. The frightening thing was how little effect it seemed to have—it was a huge knife, and he swung his arm in big arcs, and yet when Wendell looked behind them, the path seemed to be closing before his eyes. The iguana could practically *see* the jungle growing. Never mind the bugs and their diseases—if he stood still long enough, would creepers twist around his ankles and orchids start rooting in his scales?

"How often do you go down this way?" asked Wendell.

"Every . . . night . . ." said Steve, panting.

"And you have to do this every time?"

"Yup."

It took about twenty minutes to get through the jungle, and then they came out on a rocky hillside. (Even the rocks were threaded with green creepers, but the really big trees couldn't seem to get a grip.) Across the low valley stood another wall of green, and sticking out of it was a rocky outcropping. Under the outcropping lay darkness, and out of the darkness, in a slow, lazy spiral, came bats.

There were hundreds of bats, maybe thousands, and more were pouring like smoke out of the cave. There were more bats than Danny had ever dreamed existed in the world. Even Wendell, who had written that report on them, had to admit that there was a big difference between *reading* that a cave might contain over a million bats and actually *seeing* them, a great cloud of wings scribbled across the sky.

"It's like the state fair . . ." said Danny. "When you're up on the Ferris wheel, and you look down, and there's all those tiny people everywhere, and there's just so *many* of them. Except it's bats, not people. But you know what I mean."

Wendell nodded. That wasn't quite it, but it was closer than anything else he could think of. There were just so *many* of them. He'd never seen so many of *anything* in one place.

It was starting to get dark, although the stream of bats showed no sign of slowing. Steve pulled out a flashlight and said "C'mon, let's go toward

the cave. I'm not trapping tonight, so it shouldn't take long."

They scrambled down the rocky slope.

When they got to the mouth of the cave, it was much larger than Wendell had expected. The bats were ten or twenty feet overhead, rushing by like a river and paying no attention to the three reptiles underneath them.

WELL... HEH...HERE WE ARE...

YUCCK!

It *stank*.

It stank worse than anything Wendell had ever smelled, even worse than the storm sewers that he and Danny had visited, and which had stood as a pinnacle of stink he'd hoped never to see equaled. The smell was eye-watering and pungent, and it crawled up inside your nose and your mouth and burned your eyes and your tear ducts and the roof of your mouth. It was like old cheese soaked in cat urine wrapped in gym socks dipped in boiled cabbage.

"You get used to it . . ." said Steve unconvincingly.

Wendell couldn't think of anything he wanted to do less. It was an *epic* stench. If you could get used to this, you'd probably never be able to smell anything again. If the world ever ended, it would probably smell like this.

"The air's so bad in some bat caves that you can't go very deep into them," said the researcher. "This one's not quite that bad— I mean, it won't *kill* you."

WE'LL ONLY WISH WE WERE DEAD . . .

"Ready to go on?" Steve shined a light into the cave. "It's worth it, really. Well, it's actually pretty gross and a little spooky, but—"

There were few descriptions that could have gotten Danny to walk willingly into that smell, but that was one of them. Wendell followed, partly out of curiosity, mostly because the light was going deeper into the cave, and standing around in the stinky dark with the unseen jungle all around him was even worse.

The ground turned strangely crunchy underfoot. Wendell tried to see what he was walking on, but the flashlight was bobbing around too much.

"What's on the ground?" Danny wanted to know.

"The reason I had you wear boots," said Steve, and shined the light across the floor.

The floor was *alive.*

It seethed with life. Wiggly crawly things squirmed and roiled, and big dark beetles crawled over them. Danny had seen a trash bag split open

midsummer once, and there had been squirmy bits, but this was a squirmy bit the size of a parking lot.

Wendell clamped both hands over his mouth and felt his stomach heave.

"They're called guano beetles," said Steve. "They eat all the bat poop that falls from the ceiling. There are a couple million bats, so that's . . . well, a lot of poop."

"They're a good thing, really. I mean, it's gross, I know, but if they didn't do it, the poop would be over our heads. They actually keep the cave clean."

DERMESTID BEETLES. THEY'RE MEAT-EATERS. THEY EAT ANY BATS THAT FALL OFF THE CEILING. THEY'D EAT OUR FEET IF WE WEREN'T WEARING BOOTS.

...

WHY DOES EVERYTHING IN THIS JUNGLE INVOLVE ME LOSING BODY PARTS?!

Steve turned the flashlight away from the floor and played it across the ceiling. It was alive too, with the furry bodies of bats. They clung to the stone roof, flapping their leathery wings. Some of them hung motionless, apparently resting, while others launched themselves into the air and flew toward the cave entrance.

After the horrifying spectacle of the cave floor, the bats looked positively friendly. A number of them were cuddling together, wings wrapped around each other, and others were happily grooming each other's ears.

"There's a couple of different species here," said

Steve. "I've been trapping samples of . . . hmm. *That's* odd."

"Odd?" asked Danny.

"The bats are coming back in," said Steve, puzzled. "They don't usually do that until sunrise." He pointed up, and indeed, bats were streaming back into the cave, circling over their heads and landing on the walls.

MAYBE
WE SHOULD GET OUT
OF HERE!

"Yeah . . ." said Steve. "Yeah, let's get out of the cave." He followed them, still craning his neck up at the bats. "Something's scaring them. Maybe there's an owl or some other predator just outside . . ."

The humid jungle air tasted wonderful. Wendell sucked in a lungful, promptly inhaled a gnat, and doubled over coughing.

"Do you hear that?" asked Steve.

"I think he just swallowed

a bug," said Danny, pounding on the iguana's back.

"No, not Wendell. It's a kind of . . . crashing noise. I wonder if somebody's cutting trees."

"At *night*?"

"Illegal logging is a big problem out here," said Steve. "The wood's worth a lot of money. Listen, it's getting louder."

Danny listened. Once he straightened up, so did Wendell.

"I think it's coming closer," said Danny.

Steve nodded.

Wendell listened as hard as he could. The jungle made a lot of sounds at dusk, all squawks and buzzes and chirps and hums, but the crashing did seem to be getting closer.

Funny thing . . . all those jungle noises were dying away too, the closer it got. And the trees were rattling and rustling and swaying, as if there was a very small localized windstorm.

"It sounds *big,*" Wendell said.

"The bats have all gone," said Steve, sounding a little lost. Wendell gulped. Steve was a grown-up, and grown-ups weren't supposed to sound like that.

*Something* burst out of the trees.

Danny's first thought was that maybe it *was* something to do with logging, or maybe construction, because it was huge. It wasn't an animal sort of huge, it was the huge he associated with cranes and bulldozers and building equipment. The elephants at the zoo were big, but this was the size of a house, and it wasn't moving like anything he'd ever seen.

Then it stepped forward, and he thought of a gorilla the size of a building, like King Kong, because that was how it moved, big shoulders and arms crashing down, and smaller hindquarters swinging forward.

Except that it wasn't a gorilla.

"Holy crud," breathed Danny, "it's a *bat*."

# THE DRAGON-NAPPING

The bat was the biggest creature Danny had ever seen, at least on land. He'd seen a whale once, and it had been bigger, but it had been in the water. This thing looked much too large to be real, certainly too large to *move*, as if it should fall over when it tried to take a step.

It seemed to walk on its wings, its little hind legs barely touching the ground. ("Little" was a relative term. Each one was bigger than Danny's dad.)

It was hard to make out details in the late evening light, but when it turned its head, it looked

almost exactly like the false vampire bat Steve had shown them—only a thousand times larger.

"*Camazotz . . .*" breathed Steve.

A few late bats were still swirling out of the cave entrance. The giant bat snapped at them, apparently hungry. The bats fled.

Frustrated, the monster lifted its head and let out a shrill squeaky roar. It was an absurd noise to come out of a body that size. It sounded like a lion inhaling helium.

Danny couldn't help it. He laughed.

The giant bat heard him.

Its head jerked down, the fleshy pad on the end of its muzzle wiggling, the sailboat-sized ears swiveling. Danny stopped laughing immediately.

WE'RE GONNA DIE...

DANNY!

Camazotz peered at Danny and squeaked thoughtfully. It was holding him in one of its hind paws, and the grip was tight but not painful. Its claws were blunt and had cuticles an inch thick. There was coarse hair over the fingers.

Everybody said to wear gloves when handling bats, but apparently it didn't matter when the bat was handling *you*.

"Squeak?" Danny tried. "Errr . . . no habla squeak?"

It made a noise somewhere between a growl and a chitter, like a bus trying to purr. Danny didn't know if that was Giant Batspeak for "Hi!" or "I will enjoy devouring you with ketchup."

The big leaf-shaped pad on the end of its nose was almost as big as Danny, and its nostrils looked like subway tunnels. He could see the edges of enormous teeth protruding from under the lips.

The teeth didn't bother Danny that much—he had lots of relatives with enormous teeth—but the wet, cavernous nostrils were kind of disturbing. It had a booger halfway up one the size of a small dog.

The bat tilted its head thoughtfully. Its jaws yawned open.

*Well, this is how I die, I guess,* thought Danny. On the one hand, he didn't really *want* to die, but on the other hand, being eaten by a giant bat out of legend was certainly an interesting way to go.

A tongue the size of a beach towel came out and licked him.

Camazotz made a high-pitched noise, almost like a giggle, and turned. Danny clutched at the foot holding him as the world lurched.

The bat monster entered the trees, carrying the dragon into the jungle.

On the slope below the bat cave, Steve and Wendell stared after them.

"Look at it!" cried Steve. "It's walking on its wings—well, that makes sense, it's far too big to fly, and the wings are so much stronger, so it's using them like legs, and its feet are like its hands! That's amazing!"

"*Do something!*" yelled Wendell.

"I *am* doing something! I'm taking notes!"

"Oh. Um." Steve bit his lip. "Oh, *maaaaaan . . .*"

"What? What?" asked Wendell.

CALL THE ARMY! CALL THE NATIONAL GUARD! CALL THE GREEN BERETS!

AND TELL THEM WHAT, EXACTLY?

EXCUSE ME, YOU DON'T KNOW ME, BUT A GIANT BAT MONSTER JUST CARRIED OFF MY COUSIN AND I NEED YOU TO SEND HELICOPTERS?!

The iguana and the feathered reptile stared at each other for a minute, then stared out into the dark jungle and the trail of ruined trees left by Camazotz.

"We'll go back to the research station," said Steve. "There are better flashlights there, and rope, and I've got a map of the area. The bat's left a pretty big trail. We'll follow it. It has to stop moving at dawn to go to sleep."

Wendell stared hopelessly into the jungle. The insect and animals noises that had fallen silent were beginning to buzz and squawk and rattle again.

"We'll get him back," Steve said. "I promise."

# BAT MONSTER MAMA

"It's going to eat him," moaned Wendell.

"It's not going to eat him," said Steve.

"It'll *eat* him," Wendell insisted. "It'll eat him, and poop him out, and then guano beetles the size of *cars* will eat him."

Steve paused, struck by the vividness of this imagery. "It's really not likely. I mean, I don't think . . ."

"I will never have a friend like him again. No one will sit with me at lunch. Big Eddy will squash me—I'll die alone in the boys' bathroom and no one will notice."

"You know, I don't think it will."

Steve hitched a coil of rope over his shoulder. "Bats don't usually carry food around. They eat it on the spot, because it's hard to fly otherwise. And it didn't eat Danny right there. In fact, from the noises it was making . . . No, that's crazy."

**109**

WHAT? WHAT?

WELL, IT WAS MAKING NOISES AT HIM ALMOST LIKE A MOTHER BAT WHEN IT GROOMS A BABY...

"And it—she—thinks Danny's her *baby*?"

"Well, maybe. But that's a good thing!"

You could have cut Wendell's skepticism with a knife.

"If she thinks he's her baby, she won't eat him. And she probably won't drop him, or squish him, or leave him to get eaten by jaguars."

Wendell hadn't even *considered* jaguars.

HE'S DOOMED.

"Come on," said Steve. "We're going after him. Camazotz has to have a roost somewhere. We just have to follow her trail back to it and wait until daylight, when she'll come back to sleep. Then we can grab him."

"Oh good," said Wendell. "We're doomed too."

So far, Danny did not feel particularly doomed.

What he mostly felt was seasick.

Clutched in a hind paw as Danny was, every step Camazotz took was a vast swinging *lurch.* It wasn't straight, either—he slipped side to side, depending on which arm Camazotz was leading with. Occasionally the giant bat got tired of carrying him and switched hind paws, which involved being airborne and then briefly squished.

This did nothing for the seasickness.

*This is a great adventure,* he told himself. He'd been captured by ninja frogs and giant squid, but never by a Zapotec bat monster before.

He would have enjoyed it a lot more if he hadn't been in danger of throwing up. Or if he had any idea where Camazotz was taking him.

He'd tried to see where they were going, but it was a blur of shadows and greenery, and it was going in all directions, which was really hard to watch. So he kept his eyes shut tight, feeling the fur of the giant bat's belly against the back of his head, and concentrated on keeping his lunch down.

He'd also tried to breathe fire at first. But his stomach had just made a perilous *glurrrrrch* noise and threatened to bring up something a lot more solid than flame.

He was so busy *not* throwing up that it was a shock when they stopped moving.

Camazotz stood on the edge of a river. It looked like the same one that Steve had boated up, but Danny couldn't be sure. The moon had come out, and reflected a white wash across the water.

Very carefully, the bat set him down on the bank, and then hunkered down itself beside him.

Danny brushed himself off and looked up at the face of the bat. "Um. Thank you for letting me go?"

Camazotz made a cheerful squeaking noise, leaned down, and licked him again. Danny winced.

Then the giant bat leaned out over the water and stared deeply into it.

Danny rubbed the back of his neck. "Um," he said.

The bat ignored him.

Had it lost interest? Should he make a run for it? Could he get away?

Probably not.

Maybe he could sort of sneak away, very quietly—Camazotz hadn't noticed him until he'd laughed. He could hide under a bush or something until it went away . . .

He slid a glance at the bat and took a casual step away.

The bat continued to ignore him.

He tried another step.

With terrifying speed for something so huge, the bat slammed its entire face into the water. Danny let out a noise that was absolutely, positively *not* a shriek and jumped at least another foot in the air.

Camazotz lifted its face out of the river. A gigantic fish, longer than Danny was tall, flopped from its jaws.

It wolfed the fish down as casually as Danny

might eat a chicken nugget, and went back to staring into the water.

"Oh . . . kay . . ." said Danny, taking another step back. Apparently he wasn't on the menu, which was comforting, but not by very much.

He was about ten steps from the tree line. He gulped.

Camazotz looked over at him and made another cheery squeak, like a subway train trying to make friends.

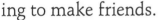 

Danny froze.

He wished Wendell were here. Wendell would have puked all over the jungle and he couldn't run as fast as Danny and he would *definitely* have blamed Danny for everything, but at least the dragon wouldn't have been alone.

And Wendell knew something about bats. That might have been helpful. Steve would have been even more helpful, but then Wendell would be stuck in the jungle all by himself, and it wasn't any good to get rescued from a giant bat only to discover that Wendell had been sat on by an endangered tapir.

Another sudden splash and another fish. This time, though, Camazotz picked it up with one foot, turned, and held it out to Danny.

"Um," said Danny.

He'd eaten a piece of sushi once, at a restaurant with his parents. It had been interesting, in a not-sure-if-he-liked-it kind of way. There was a *big* difference between a little tube of rice with a bit of pink meat in the middle and a whole dead fish being dangled over his head.

"Err. Thank you. No."

The bat waved the fish at him again.

He held up both hands and pushed it back, turning his face away.

Camazotz shrugged its wings and tossed the fish into its mouth, then went back into the water.

*I've got to get out of here before it decides to try to feed me something else,* Danny thought, and backed another step toward the jungle.

Halfway there now. He glanced into the trees. It was incredibly dark and tangled, but surely it would be easier for *him* to move through it than Camazotz.

Just a few more steps.

Just a few more . . .

# THE ROOST

"Are you sure this is the right way?" asked Wendell.

"As sure as I was five minutes ago," said Steve.

Camazotz had cut a swath of destruction in bent and broken trees, forming a path that was relatively easy to follow, but it wasn't a *straight* path. It wandered around, as the giant bat had found something interesting or tasty, and sometimes there were large gaps in it, where the bat leaped or scrambled over something it couldn't knock down. Steve and Wendell had spent twenty minutes wandering around in a gap, and Wendell still wasn't entirely convinced they hadn't come out on their own back trail going the wrong way.

The problem was that the jungle all looked alike. It was dark and dripping and full of groaning and flapping and buzzing, some of which might be bugs or birds and some of which might be jaguars or . . . or . . . iguana-eating tapirs or something. After all, if a two-story bat god could live out here for years, without being noticed by a bat researcher practically in its backyard, there could be *anything*. Ancient primitive dinosaurs. Lost tribes of cannibals. Things that nobody knew the name of because nobody who saw it had ever lived to say anything but *"Oh god, not my spleen—!"*

"We just follow this back to Camazotz's roost," said Steve. "She has to come back to her roost by daybreak. And then we get Danny back."

"What if she has more than one roost?"

"Then we cry a lot," said Steve.

This did not strike Wendell as helpful.

They kept walking. The ground was full of mud and holes and tree roots, and Wendell kept smacking his shins into things. The iguana's only consolation was that he was doused in bug spray.

(He considered the slight wooziness and difficulty breathing to be a small price to pay for total insect coverage.)

"We can't be too far away," said Steve, sounding much too hopeful and not nearly confident enough, as far as Wendell was concerned. "She showed up right at dusk. The roost *has* to be nearby."

Wendell was about to reply, but a leaf-covered branch slapped him in the face. He pawed bark off his tongue. "Yeech!"

He was still trying to get the taste of tree out of his mouth when the path widened and began to look less like a newly broken trail and more like a clearing.

"See?" cried Steve. "There!"

"Now what do we do?" asked Wendell. The cave looked very large and very dark.

"We look inside," said Steve. "Then we hide and wait for Camazotz and Danny to come home."

Some miles away, as the false vampire bat flies, Danny was wishing very much that he was home. Waiting for Camazotz to turn its head so he could finish moving into the jungle was excruciating. It combined the very worst parts of boredom and terror. He didn't dare move until Camazotz was distracted, and he didn't dare take his eyes off the bat, which was just sitting there staring into the water and occasionally glancing up at him.

Bats were fascinating-looking, and Camazotz was gigantic and monstrous and thus even *more* fascinating, but after half an hour, Danny was getting tired of looking at it.

He wished he'd brought his comic book, *Single-Cell Samurai.* He was so busy thinking about bacteria assassins that when the strike came, Danny almost missed his chance. Camazotz had thrown its head back and was wolfing down the fish, using a wing claw to shove the wiggling morsel deeper into its mouth. The fish was halfway down before Danny's brain reacted—*Oh yeah, that's what we were waiting for, let's go!*

It occurred to Danny that running blindly through the jungle, while a good start, lacked something as a long-term plan.

If he could stay in sight of the river, just inside the trees, maybe he could make his way along it. Sooner or later, he'd hit either Steve's research station, or at least the dock where Steve had picked them up.

The notion of walking miles through the jungle at night wasn't exactly pleasant, but explorers did that sort of thing all the time, didn't they? And this was Mexico, which had a population of . . . well, some really large number, anyway. Mr. Snaug had given them a test on it. Unfortunately he'd gotten a C on the test, but anyway, the point was that Mexico was a perfectly civilized country, and if he walked far enough, he'd probably come out in a Wal-Mart parking lot.

An alarmed squeaking rose from the direction of the river. Camazotz had noticed his absence.

Biting his lip, Danny began creeping along, trying to keep an eye on the river through the trees on his left. It wasn't easy. Visibility in the jungle was measured in inches.

And it was dark. Really dark. Plus, there were all these noises—noises that were probably bugs, but didn't sound like any bugs Danny had ever heard, even at summer camp, which was out in what he had previously thought of as "the deep woods."

ZEEP ZEEP KREEK-KREEK CRIK CRIK CRIK
CRIK CRIK CRIK
CHIRP CHIRP CHIRP
BUZZZZZZZzzzz
CRIK CRIK CRIK
ZZZEEP! CHIRRRK!

Then an even more alarming noise replaced the bugs—the sounds of crashing trees. Camazotz was coming.

Danny rolled under a bush, put his arms over his head, and tried to become invisible.

Luck—or something—was with him. The bat monster passed so closely by that Danny could have reached out and touched

a wing—but it didn't see him. The crashing grew fainter, and was swallowed by the jungle.

The dragon heaved a sigh that seemed to come from the bottom of his toes. He was free.

Lost, but free.

He made his way back toward the river, and began walking.

# LAIR TREASURES

Camazotz's lair was not as interesting as Wendell had hoped.

It was possible he'd been breathing dragon dandruff too long, but he'd secretly expected the monster to have a hoard, full of fabulous Aztec gold and crystal skulls and glittering obsidian knives.

Instead, it had a cave. There were rocks in it. There was nothing particularly special about the rocks, although Wendell discovered, by tripping over one, that they *were* fabulously pointy.

On the other hand, it also wasn't as bad as he'd

feared. Apparently there was only the one bat, and it went to the bathroom somewhere else. His visions of guano beetles the size of Volkswagens were not confirmed. The floor was dry and rocky. There was a cave spider in one corner, which was large and terrifying, but at least on a scale that Wendell understood.

"Fascinating . . ." said Steve, shining his light over the cave floor. "This must be it—look, she's been shedding."

Wendell had a hard time getting excited over hunks of bat hair, especially with the spider glaring at him. It had a *lot* of legs, and almost as many eyes.

It occurred to Wendell, not for the first time, that Steve had really *odd* priorities.

"The *pottery*?"

"Zapotec, I think! They must have been feeding it, giving it offerings. These are incredibly old. Wendell, this really *is* Camazotz!"

AS OPPOSED TO JUST SOME RANDOM BAT MONSTER THE SIZE OF A HOUSE?

"Well, either it's incredibly long-lived, or it's one of a breeding population," mused Steve. "We might be able to find others . . . I could probably get a grant . . ." He stepped forward, toward where the back of the cave vanished into darkness. "This is obviously a cave they've been using for centuries—I wonder if there are bones down below? A complete skeleton would be very useful—or there might even be more bats—"

"We don't need *more* giant bats right now!" snapped Wendell.

"Oh, right, right. Don't really have the equipment for caving anyway. . . . Well, let's see." Steve played the light over the walls. The cave spider retreated sulkily into a crevice, and Steve's gaze sharpened.

"Hmm. . . . Well, I couldn't fit in there. You might be able to . . . looks like it opens up a bit . . ." Steve pushed the flashlight into the crack and played it around. "Ah, looks like it joins the outside. Probably was part of the main entrance, and then a rock fell."

"I'm *not* going in there," said Wendell. "And shouldn't we be hiding outside anyway?"

"Right, right." Steve gave a last longing look at the cave. "I can always come back . . ."

They scrambled back down the hillside, looking for hiding places, while the moon sank coldly overhead.

Danny was lost.

He was also soggy and unhappy and he'd stepped into some kind of mud and lost one of his boots. This was not the sort of adventure he preferred. Ideally he liked adventures that had moderate peril, only minor injury, and ended quickly, not ones that dragged on and on and squelched underfoot. And ideally, Wendell would be along too. Adventures weren't nearly as much fun if there was no one to be suitably impressed by your dragony bravery.

So when a massive scaly head dropped from a tree directly in front of him, he staggered back a step, shocked, and then broke into a broad grin of delight.

"Um. . . ." It was a boa constrictor. It looked a little like Ms. Brown the English teacher, only much bigger. It might even be an anaconda.

"HISSSSS!"

It occurred to Danny that the anaconda did not look helpful. In fact, it looked angry about something.

And come to think of it, it wasn't wearing clothes . . . Ms. Brown always wore a tube sweater and big dangly necklaces. And she never hissed. She would have considered hissing to be terribly bad grammar. If she caught you passing notes, she might demand that you "read it to the whole classsss," but that was as far as she went.

"Um . . . Do you speak English?"

The anaconda struck.

Danny yelped and dropped flat, and the giant snake passed overhead and slammed into a tree trunk.

Maybe it wasn't a person after all. Maybe it was a primitive *animal* snake.

The snake whipped around, looking downright furious, with scuffed scales across its nose.

As he scrambled toward the river, trying to get away, Danny's only clear thought—and it wasn't very—was that he was glad Ms. Brown wasn't here to see this.

PIRANHAS OR SNAKE— DON'T MAKE ME CHOOSE!

Danny had never been so glad to see the underside of a giant bat monster in his life.

The snake, clearly overmatched, whipped into the undergrowth like a traumatized shoelace and was gone. Camazotz picked Danny up in a claw and held him up to eye level.

Camazotz gave him a thorough sniffing, and Danny thought he would be sucked into its giant nostrils. Luckily, the bat seemed satisfied after several sniffs, let out a happy chitter, and gave Danny another sloppy lick across the face. Danny groaned.

Oh well, better that it be happy than angry with him for trying to escape. Danny decided that escaping into the jungle wasn't such a good idea. There were monsters out there other than Camazotz. The bat monster didn't seem inclined to eat him—yet—and maybe it would return to Steve's bat cave, or at least someplace Danny recognized.

Camazotz shifted Danny to its other claw and looked up at the sky. It chattered again, sounding almost thoughtful, and then began making its way up the river, back the way they had come.

# WAITING AND WAITING

"I itch," said Wendell.

"So do I," said Steve. "There's not much we can do about it."

Wendell sighed.

The two of them were hiding in some large bushes at the base of the rocky hill where Camazotz roosted, and it was desperately uncomfortable. The bushes had long, arrowhead-shaped leaves with pointy ends that jabbed into you no matter how you shifted or wiggled. The stems had a fine fuzz that looked soft and turned out to be prickly, and if they hadn't been sitting in Wendell's cloud of bug spray, they would probably have been eaten alive by the locals.

Wendell could see some of the bugs lurking around the edges. They looked like ants, but they were bigger than any ant he'd ever seen, and they were clacking their mandibles in a distinctly unfriendly fashion.

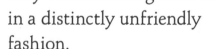

"It shouldn't be much longer now," said Steve hopefully. "It's starting to get light out."

The feathered dragon was right. The sky was now murky gray instead of black, and there was a weak, bruised-looking light on the eastern horizon.

Wendell opened his mouth to say something, and closed it again. He'd heard something. A thumping? The footfall of a distant monster?

It came again, and again, and then he was sure. Steve caught his eye and nodded frantically, putting a claw over his snout to signal they should be silent.

So they waited, hardly breathing, while the crashing came nearer, until it was almost on top of them. Wendell forgot all about the itching and the prickly bush as Camazotz burst from the tree line and began climbing up the hill.

Steve craned his neck. So did Wendell. Did it have—was that, in its back claws—yes!

Wendell hit Steve's arm excitedly. Steve nodded vigorously.

It was Danny.

The giant bat climbed up the hillside toward the cave. At the mouth, it paused, its back to them, and then folded its wings up carefully. It seemed to become a great deal smaller—the size of a semi-truck, rather than a house—and climbed into the hole.

"Now what?" whispered Wendell.

"Danny's inside the cave," Steve whispered back. "We just wait until she falls asleep, and then we can go get him."

They waited. The sun got higher and the ants got more restless and the bush seemed to get even more prickly, although that might have been Wendell's imagination.

"Now?"

"Not yet."

It was boring. It was really boring. Wendell poked at one of the ants with a twig and the ant grabbed the end in its jaws and sheared it in half. The iguana stifled a yelp.

"Good thing about the bug spray, huh?" muttered Steve.

They waited some more.

"Now?"

"Not yet."

At last, when Wendell thought he couldn't wait another minute, Steve stood up and said, "Now. Stay quiet."

They made their way up the hillside as sneakily as possible. This was difficult while wearing large rubber boots, and even more difficult for Wendell, who was not one of nature's naturally sneaky people. If there was a dry twig anywhere in a five-mile radius, Wendell could be relied upon to step on it, and then probably fall over and shriek.

SNAP

RUSTLE

THUD!

Whenever they looked up at the cave, all they could see was the furred back of Camazotz.

"She must roost lying down," murmured Steve. "Of course, she doesn't fly, so there's no reason to hang upside down if she doesn't have to . . . and there can't be many caves big enough to hang upside down in. Still, I would have thought . . ."

"Never mind that," said Wendell, "how are we going to get past her?"

Steve's tail twitched. "I'm . . . not sure."

They reached the mouth of the cave, and stared at each other in helpless dismay.

Camazotz's back filled the entire entrance. It had clearly lain down with its back in the mouth of the cave, and unless they actually climbed over it, there was no way in.

"Well," said Steve, "that's not entirely true. There's still a way in . . ."

Wendell followed his gaze to the mouth of the spider-infested crevice. "Oh, *no.*"

"You'd have to go alone," said Steve. "But you can get Danny and you can both squeeze out. I'll give you a flashlight."

"There are spiders in there!"

"*Danny's* in there," said Steve with ruthless logic.

Wendell stuffed a hand in his mouth and bit it in terror.

"You can do it," said Steve. "You have to do it."

Wendell knew, in his heart of hearts, that he was a coward. And he was okay with that. Danny needed somebody to say "If we do that, we're going to die," and occasionally he even listened. They were best friends. They had a system. Danny was fearless and Wendell was terrified, and it worked out between them.

But at the moment, what his best friend needed wasn't a coward. It was somebody to take the flashlight and say: "Okay, I'll do it."

There was nobody else in the world he would have done it for. (Well, maybe his mom, but his mom wasn't in the habit of getting stuck in the lairs of bat monsters.) Wendell took a deep breath, squared his shoulders, and reached for Steve's flashlight.

OKAY. I'LL DO IT.

# A CRY FOR HELP

Danny was sitting in the dark, being bored.

There was a faint glimmering of light around the edges of Camazotz's fur, but not enough to allow Danny to see much of the cave, except that it got very deep and dark at the back. He kept tripping over roundish things that clattered like crockery, and there didn't seem to be any way to escape.

He would have considered going into the darkness at the back of the cave, but the memory of the crawling beetle floor of Steve's cave was still fresh in his mind.

Meanwhile, Camazotz was snoring like a locomotive. The snores echoed through the cave and made it hard for Danny to hear himself think.

The dragon had just about decided that the only thing left to do was find a warm patch of giant bat to lean on and try to get some sleep when the light seemed to get brighter, and he heard a familiar voice go "Hssst!"

WENDELL?

The iguana's face stared at him over a flashlight beam. "Get me out of here! It's too small and I think I'm stuck and there's all these spiders and the bug spray isn't working and one of them is looking at me and there's something with lots of legs on my tail and *I want out!*"

Wendell came free like a foot out of a crusty sneaker—slowly, and with grimy streaks. Danny was so happy to see his friend that he could have hugged him, but Wendell was too busy dancing around and flailing at imaginary spiders on his head. Danny helped him yank off the last of the cobwebs.

I CAN'T BELIEVE YOU FOUND ME!

WELL, THE GIANT BAT MONSTER WAS HARD TO MISS . . .

NOW WE CAN GET OUT OF HERE!

"Oh no!" Wendell shuddered. "I'm *not* going back through that hole. That was worse than going to the dentist. The dentist doesn't have spiders."

"Then how else are we going to get out?"

Wendell turned the flashlight toward the back of the cave. "Maybe the cave comes out somewhere near the bottom of the hill."

Danny looked back at the crevice. It did look pretty tight . . .

Camazotz snuffled in its sleep. That was enough. Flashlight at the ready, Wendell and Danny hurried deeper into the cave.

It was dark.

It was not quite as dark as the bottom of the ocean, but it was darker than a storm sewer, and much darker than a closet, or the bathroom when you needed a drink of water late at night.

They spent a few minutes recounting what had happened—Danny was surprised to learn that Camazotz was probably a girl, and (bleck!) thought she was his mom, and Wendell was suit-

ably horrified by Danny's encounter with the anaconda. But their voices seemed squeezed out under
the weight of the dark.

Fortunately, it was a very large tunnel. The floor
was rough and broken, but at least they weren't running into any walls. Camazotz could have walked
through here. Danny wondered why she didn't.

They didn't see anything that might be a way
out—but as Danny was sweeping the flashlight
in front of them, something glittered.

"What's that?" asked Wendell.

"I don't know. It looks like metal . . ."

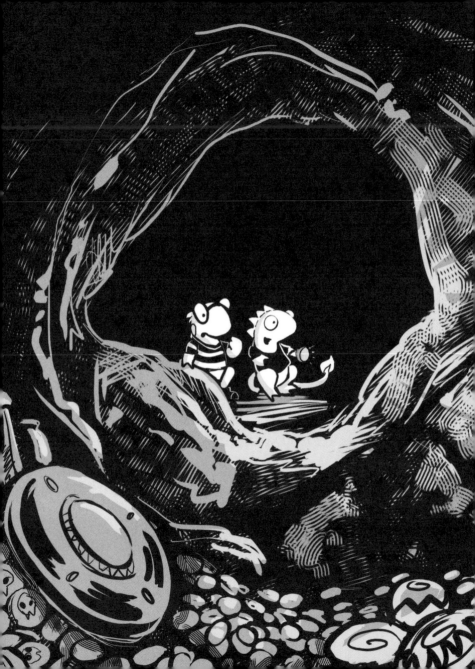

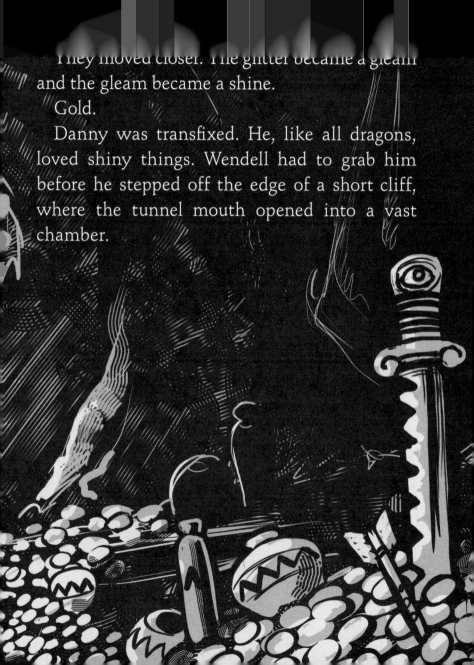

They moved closer. The glitter became a gleam and the gleam became a shine.

Gold.

Danny was transfixed. He, like all dragons, loved shiny things. Wendell had to grab him before he stepped off the edge of a short cliff, where the tunnel mouth opened into a vast chamber.

Gold covered the floor—shields and scabbards and disks and daggers and knives and necklaces. The flashlight's beam was caught by the gold and reflected back at them in a rippling sea of light.

"Now this," said Danny in awe, "this is a *hoard*."

Wendell looked at his friend. The dragon was transfixed with the purest of pure greed.

DRAGONS...

"You can't carry it," he growled. "And it probably belongs to somebody. The Zapotec gave it to the bat."

"Then it belongs to the bat! The bat isn't using it! The bat doesn't care!" Danny waved his hands in the air, making the flashlight beam zigzag wildly over the ceiling. "Besides, I don't want all of it! Just . . . y'know . . . a little gold. Not much. Camazotz'll never miss it."

"There was gold back up top if you really want

it," said Wendell, annoyed. "We don't have to climb down there. How would we get back up? And I don't see a way out."

"Out . . ." said Danny distantly, clearly not hearing a word Wendell was saying. He swept the flashlight over the tide of golden offerings again. He was going to be rich. He was going to have a hoard that was the envy of every dragon on the continent. Oh, probably his parents would make him put most of it into savings, but they'd leave him a few pieces—they weren't unreasonable—and he'd probably even give one to Mom, that would be even better than a butterfly named after you, and . . .

Something moved.

Far back in the cave, a shape that Wendell had thought was a rock formation unfolded itself from the ceiling.

It was another bat. Another Camazotz.

Wendell knew Danny was looking at the gold and didn't see the monster, and he knew that he should scream or grab his friend or shout a warn-

ing or *something.* But his mind was running in little gibbering circles and for some reason, all he could think was: *Steve was wrong. They* do *sleep hanging upside down sometimes.*

Nothing that big should be that silent. The bat put a wing tip down on the floor and slowly flipped itself over. In that huge room, it should have looked small, but instead it looked even bigger than *their* Camazotz.

Danny swept the flashlight over a particularly fine golden shield and made appreciative noises. Wendell could only see the edge of the monster now, the long folds of the wings, and the gleam of enormous eyes.

EEEP

"This is the find of the century!" said Danny. "I'll never fit it all under my mattress. I might need a bigger bed . . ."

Wendell said, somewhat louder, "Eeeep!"

"What?" Danny gave him an annoyed look. "Do you need to go to the bathroom or something?"

The monster lunged.

It broke Wendell's paralysis. He grabbed Danny's shoulder and flung them both backward into the cave mouth.

"Whaa—*crud!!*"

The flashlight spun out of Danny's hands and bounced down the drop, throwing crazy shadows. The bat closed the gap between them like a racehorse.

"RUN!" screamed Wendell, who turned to do so himself and promptly fell flat on his face.

COME ON!

The bat slammed into the stone. Jaws snapped an inch from their faces, and warm, foul-smelling spit sprayed across their skin. Wendell shrieked. The bat chattered savagely at them, a horrible staticky noise that Wendell felt with his whole body, not just his ears.

The second Camazotz was indeed stuck. The opening was too small for its shoulders to fit through the hole.

But its wing tips could fit. It shot one, a great leathery mass with a scythe-like claw at the end, and slashed at them. Danny fell flat and yanked Wendell down with him.

The wing clawed futilely at the air over their heads, then pulled back. The head of the second Camazotz appeared again, snaking into the corridor and snapping its jaws.

I DON'T *THINK* SHE'LL EAT US.

YOU DON'T *THINK?*

WELL, SHE WAS NICE. YOU KNOW. FOR A GIANT BAT MONSTER.

Danny was remembering Big Eddy at the pool. The bully couldn't beat him up if there were grown-ups there. If he could get *his* Camazotz down there—

"Camazotz!" he yelled. "Camazotz, *help!*"

"You've lost your mind," said Wendell. "I know I say that a lot, but really this time—"

The second Camazotz clawed at the tunnel. The hillside shook, dust starting to come down in earnest, with bits of stinging gravel. Where was his Camazotz? Was she still asleep? Did she not come down here?

SHE THINKS I'M HER BABY, RIGHT?

WELL, THAT'S WHAT STEVE SAID...

Danny stopped his wailing long enough to hiss, "If you ever tell another living soul about this, I'll tell them you sleep with a stuffed bunny named Mr. Higgins!"

"You leave Mr. Higgins out of this!"

Danny took another breath. Was the crying helping? Did the bat hear him? Would she respond?

And then, suddenly, there was a rumbling squeak. Danny turned.

He had time enough to register that it wasn't as dark in the cave as it should have been without the flashlight, before the light was blotted out. A moment later, a familiar claw grabbed him around the middle, and lifted him up.

The light was coming from the entrance to the cave. It was definitely after dawn. Camazotz had grabbed them both, one in each claw. She leaned down and sniffed Danny, then gave him a brief lick.

Another spate of chattering came from farther down the tunnel, and then the sounds of claws battering on stone. The whole hillside seemed to shake, and dust drifted down from the ceiling.

Apparently she did. The giant bat set them down in the mouth of the cave, gave Danny another lick, and turned back down the tunnel. There was another burst of furious static, and the hillside shook as if a bus had run into it.

Camazotz took a step down the tunnel, toward the other bat monster.

"Come on!" hissed Wendell. "Let's get out of here!"

Danny looked after Camazotz. "I—but—I don't want her to get hurt!"

SHE WEIGHS LIKE FIFTY BAZILLION TONS! SHE'LL BE FINE!

THE OTHER ONE'S BIGGER THAN SHE IS!

THEY'RE MONSTERS!

SHE WAS NICE.

"Let's get out of here! This place is shaking, and I don't know what that noise is—"

Danny grabbed his sleeve. "Steve, there's another one! Down there! It's stuck in the cave, and our Camazotz is going after it."

Steve looked ready to start down the tunnel and watch, but Wendell blocked them both, waving his arms. "There's no way we can possibly stop them! Let's just get out of here before we get squished or eaten or both!"

I GUESS . . .

I SUPPOSE WE CAN ALWAYS COME BACK . . .

Another chittering roar came from the tunnel, and was met with chittering from Camazotz.

"She sounds annoyed," said Danny.

"I'm sure she can handle it," said Steve.

Wendell had given up on both of them and was halfway out of the cave already.

There was another sound, a leathery *boom!* as if somebody had just been slapped upside the head with a wing the size of a barn door, and then a yelp. Somehow, Danny didn't think it came from *his* Camazotz.

"Sounds like she has the situation under control," said Steve.

"Yeah . . ." Danny remembered how she had dealt with the anaconda.

"We should probably go."

"Yeah."

# DRAGONBAT

The return to Steve's research station seemed to take forever—probably because while Wendell kept looking behind him to make sure they weren't being followed, he accidentally walked through another spiderweb. He spent the rest of the trip trying to paw invisible webs off him and shuddering, while Danny told Steve about the night he'd had. (Danny would have felt worse about Wendell and the spiderweb if Wendell hadn't been making "waaaah!" noises at him and snickering. When he got home, Mr. Higgins was going to get strapped to a bottle rocket and become the first stuffed bunny in space.)

He was very glad to see Steve's house, though. Even if the bats could have ripped the door right off, there was something comforting about having a layer of wood between him and the jungle.

Steve got them both some hot chocolate and wandered around the room, muttering to himself.

THE OTHER BAT MUST BE CAMAZOTZ'S MATE.

"If he grew too big to get out of the roost, she's probably been feeding him." Steve took a slug of hot cocoa. "That's not unheard of. Vampire bats will share blood with bats back at the roost. She probably didn't want to bring you down there, because she thought he'd eat you. Hmm, I wonder if we can get him out?"

Danny thought about what it would be like to be stuck in a cave for your entire life. It was hard to feel sorry for the second Camazotz, but in that position, he'd probably be pretty grumpy too. "Well . . . if it's for *science* . . ."

"I'm not helping you break out a giant bat monster," said Wendell grimly. "Not even for science."

**195**

"No, you're not," said Steve. "That's what unpaid interns are for. You two are getting back on a bus and going home with your little bat friend." He reached into the closet with a gloved hand and carefully detached their bat. "Looks like he ate some mealworms too."

It was a quiet ride back to the bus. The birds were still shrieking, the bugs were still buzzing, but Wendell was so tired he couldn't get up the energy to worry. If his limbs fell off, they fell off. Hopefully they'd do it quietly.

Steve waited with them until the bus arrived. Danny took the pillowcase with their bat in it, and they climbed up the steps. Wendell found a seat and collapsed into it, but Danny paused to look back at Steve.

"Will Camazotz be okay? I mean, she was pretty nice—for a giant bat monster. And the other one was awfully big . . ."

"She'll be fine," said Steve. "She's a new species

to science, and they'll protect her cave and the others near it, just in case. You and Wendell helped save her species—and my bats too." He grinned. "I think I'll call her *Camazotus dragonbreathii.*"

"Ooooh . . ." said Danny. Having a butterfly named after you was one thing, having a monster named after you—well, it just didn't get any better than that.

"Hey! Don't I get a Latin name?" Wendell appeared in the window.

"Well . . ." Steve considered. "For your undeniable bravery in going in after Danny . . . I could probably name the bat's lice after you."

IT HAD LICE?!

"Have a good trip," said Steve.

"Let us know about Camazotz," said Danny, and the bus took them away.

They slept most of the way home, at least after Wendell stopped muttering about horrible giant lice. It was nearly noon by the time they staggered into Danny's kitchen.

"You look exhausted," said Danny's mother. "Did you have a good time?"

Wendell and Danny looked at each other.

"Were you up all night?" Mrs. Dragonbreath emptied out the remains of the coffeepot.

"Yeah. Uh . . . Steve showed us the cave where he does all his bat research." That seemed safe enough. "It was really . . . um . . ."

"Exciting," said Wendell.

"Yeah."

Danny's mother looked them over, took in the dirt and the scrapes and the dark circles under their eyes. She decided that they were back safely, and beyond that, she didn't want to know. "Well, that's good. Why don't you boys go wash up, and I'll get some lunch ready for you?"

"Lunch would be *awesome*," said Danny, and went to go scrub off the bat slobber and other last remnants of the night's adventure.

That evening, just after it got dark, Danny and Wendell stood in the backyard. Danny was wearing gloves, and Wendell was hiding behind a lawn chair, just as a precaution.

"Okay, little guy," Danny said to the pillowcase. "Time to go." He opened the pillowcase.

Nothing happened.

Danny frowned, and pushed on the underside of the bag, turning it inside out until the bat was sitting on a wad of fabric in his hands. It lifted its tiny, wrinkled face and looked around.

"Go on," Danny urged. "Go . . . be a bat somewhere. There's lots of bugs."

"Tasty, tasty bugs," called Wendell from behind the lawn chair.

The bat chittered, stretched its wings, and launched itself into the air. It circled once around the lawn, a flash of brown in the porch light, and then was gone.

"Well, that's that," said Danny, dusting off his hands. "Let's go watch TV."

"There's a show about bats on the nature channel," said Wendell, grinning.

"I like bats," said Danny with dignity. "Bats are cool. I hope our bat has a great life. But I've had about enough of bats for the last few days. Is there something on with explosions or ghosts or haunted houses?"

"I'm sure we can find something," said Wendell. "We always do."

And watch
out for the
**HAUNTING**
fifth book in the
Dragonbreath series
**COMING
SOON!**

# A WORD ABOUT BATS . . .

Bats are one of the coolest—and most useful!—animals on earth. A single bat can eat over a thousand mosquitoes an hour. (That's a lot of bugs!) Many plants, including some of our favorite fruits, are pollinated by bats too. The smallest bat on earth weighs less than a penny, while some flying foxes have six-foot wingspans.

Unfortunately, bats are in trouble. People are often scared of bats, thinking they all carry rabies or will get caught in your hair. And bats have been hit hard by diseases and destruction of their home caves. So these days, bats need our help.

You can find out more cool bat facts, see photos of all kinds of weird species, and learn what to do if you find an injured bat (Hint: Always get a grown-up!) at Bat Conservation International (www.batcon.org).

YAY, BATS!